THE FIRE DRAGONS

DRAGON GIRLS

Eloise the
Flame Dragon

Maddy Mara

DRAGON GIRLS

Eloise the Flame Dragon

by Maddy Mara

Scholastic Inc.

If you purchased this book without a cover, you should be aware that this book is stolen property. It was reported as "unsold and destroyed" to the publisher, and neither the author nor the publisher has received any payment for this "stripped book."

Copyright © 2025 by Maddy Mara
Illustrations by Sara Foresti, copyright © 2025 by Scholastic Inc.

All rights reserved. Published by Scholastic Inc., *Publishers since 1920.* SCHOLASTIC and associated logos are trademarks and/or registered trademarks of Scholastic Inc.

The publisher does not have any control over and does not assume any responsibility for author or third-party websites or their content.

No part of this publication may be reproduced, stored in a retrieval system, or transmitted in any form or by any means, electronic, mechanical, photocopying, recording, or otherwise, or used to train any artificial intelligence technologies, without written permission of the publisher. For information regarding permission, write to Scholastic Inc., Attention: Permissions Department, 557 Broadway, New York, NY 10012.

This book is a work of fiction. Names, characters, places, and incidents are either the product of the author's imagination or are used fictitiously, and any resemblance to actual persons, living or dead, business establishments, events, or locales is entirely coincidental.

ISBN 978-1-339-01991-8

10 9 8 7 6 5 4 3 2 1   25 26 27 28 29

Printed in the U.S.A.   40

First printing 2025

Book design by Cassy Price

1

When the doorbell rang, Eloise jumped up. "I'll get it!" she called, running to the door. Today was her birthday and her besties, Ash and Maya, were coming over. Eloise didn't want a big fuss. For her, a little party with her friends was the perfect celebration.

At the front door, Eloise stopped. Who would arrive first? Ash was almost always on time. But then, Maya was nearly as excited as Eloise about the party. During the week at school, Maya had joked that she might just arrive an hour early. So maybe she would be first?

Well, there was only one way to find out.

Eloise flung open the door. BOTH her friends stood there, huge grins on their faces. Maya was holding a present and Ash was clutching a bunch of helium balloons.

"Happy birthday!" they chorused.

Maya put down the present in the hall and hugged Eloise tightly. Then Ash tried to hug

her, but the balloons got in the way and kept bopping Eloise in the face.

Eloise laughed as she shut the door. "You two look great, by the way."

The three of them had decided to get dressed up for the occasion. Ash was wearing a very cool blue blazer she'd gotten for her cousin's wedding. Maya was wearing her favorite sparkly red top. Eloise had chosen a fancy romper her mom had made.

Eloise led the way through to the dining area, which was warm and smelled delicious. Her mom and dad were there, arranging bowls on the table. Some bowls contained frosting in different shades. Others held candies in every possible shape, size, and flavor.

"Hi!" Eloise's parents said together.

"Now," said her mom, "it's your job to decorate these." She placed a plate of delicious-looking cupcakes in the center of the dining table.

"They look amazing," said Ash, picking one up.

"Don't they?" agreed Eloise's dad. "Eloise made them."

"Did you really?" Maya looked impressed. "Wow!"

Eloise nodded. "I did them totally on my own," she said proudly. "Except for putting them into the oven and getting them out again."

Her mom or dad always did that part. Eloise was secretly afraid of the big blast of hot air when the oven door was opened.

The three friends got busy decorating the cupcakes. Eloise's dad put on a playlist of music so they could dance while they worked.

"Frosting is an amazing invention," said Maya. "You think you can't fit one more thing on a cupcake. Then you add more frosting and voilà! You can stick on ten more things."

"Exactly," Ash said, licking her fingers. "It's like glue, but much tastier."

Eloise laughed. Ash and Maya were so funny. She always got the giggles when they were around.

Suddenly, the lights went off. Eloise looked up, surprised. Her mom was standing there holding a cake! On the top flickered a ring of candles. Her parents began to sing "Happy Birthday." Ash and Maya immediately joined in.

Eloise's dad cleared a space on the table and her mom carefully put the cake in front of her. It looked incredible! It was three layers high and covered in swirls of her favorite caramel frosting.

"Blow out the candles!" Ash said.

"And make a wish," Maya added.

Eloise did so, making the same wish she'd made for three years in a row. *I wish that the three of us will be friends forever.*

When Eloise had blown out the candles, her dad turned to Ash and Maya. "Do you want a turn?"

Ash and Maya nodded. It was tradition in Eloise's home that guests also got to blow out the candles and make a wish. Her mom produced a box of matches to relight the candles.

"Eloise, would you like to try striking the match?" she asked.

Eloise shook her head. She didn't like the way matches suddenly flared into life.

"Can I?" Ash asked. "I sometimes do it at home."

Ash managed to light two candles before the matchstick got too short. Then Maya took a turn. The first match broke in half. The second didn't light at all. Then the first two candles went out.

Maya looked in the box. "There are no more matches!"

"Come with me to the kitchen," said Eloise's dad. "We'll find some more."

"I'd better check on the pizzas in the oven," said Eloise's mom, following them.

"Oh! I left the present at the front door!" said Ash, dashing off down the hallway.

Eloise found herself alone in the darkened room. She gazed at the beautiful cake before her. She couldn't wait to have a slice.

Suddenly, the unlit candles burst back into flames. Eloise stared nervously. What was going on? Maybe they hadn't gone all the way out before? Or maybe they were those trick candles that relit? As she blinked, Eloise heard faint singing.

Magic Forest, Magic Forest, come explore...

She looked around the room. Who was singing? It wasn't her parents or friends. She could hear them clattering around in the kitchen, opening and closing drawers in the hunt for more matches. Maybe it was a song from her dad's playlist? But he'd stopped the music so they could sing "Happy Birthday." Eloise heard the song again, louder this time.

Magic Forest, Magic Forest, come explore...

The flames on the candles grew taller and kept changing color. One moment they were gold, then blue, then scarlet. These were very special candles!

Eloise leaned closer. She could see something within the flickering flames. It looked like a forest, with tall trees and birds and other animals. No heat seemed to come from the flames, although they were very big now. Instead, Eloise could feel a cool breeze ruffling her hair.

Her heart began to thump. Something big was about to happen. She opened her mouth to call out to the others but instead found herself singing along with the song. It was as if she'd known it all her life.

Magic Forest, Magic Forest, hear my roar!

The trees grew taller still, rising up out of the flames and surrounding Eloise. The breeze turned into a wind, whipping around her. Eloise closed her eyes as it grew stronger and stronger... until it lifted her off her feet!

Eloise was spun around and around until she had no idea which way was up or down or left or right. Finally, the spinning slowed and she felt herself dropping gently onto solid ground once more.

Slowly, Eloise opened her eyes. She already

knew she was no longer at home. But where was she, exactly?

All around her, trees wilted slightly in the hot, still air. Birds flew above, singing songs Eloise had never heard before. Despite the heat, she gave a little shiver. Her feet felt strange. Had she landed on them in a weird way? When she looked down, she cried out in surprise. Her feet—and her hands, for that matter—were gone! Now she had four sturdy paws covered with gleaming, metallic-gray scales. Each paw was tipped with a set of sharp claws.

In shock, Eloise tried to walk. But she instantly toppled over, landing with a loud crash on the ground.

"I must still be dizzy from all that spinning," she said to herself. Hang on, what was going on with her voice? It sounded so loud!

There was a rustling from the undergrowth. Eloise froze. She really hoped something fierce wasn't about to attack. She wanted to run away, but she didn't trust her weird new legs to carry her. The rustling grew louder and from the long grass emerged a tiny pale gray pony. On its back was a pair of wings.

"Don't worry," said the pony with a flick of its long mane. "It takes a little time adjusting to being a Dragon Girl."

Eloise stared at the pony. She wasn't sure what was more confusing—what the pony had

said, or the fact that the pony had spoken at all.

"I'm a ... Dragon Girl?" she said, choosing the first thing.

"You sure are," said the pony, trotting up beside her. "A Fire Dragon Girl, to be precise."

Eloise stood up and moved around, trying to get used to this new body. She still felt a bit odd, but also very big and powerful. She had a huge tail with a point at the end. Her neck felt extremely long. On her head, she could feel two ears that she could turn in different directions.

"Is there something stuck on my back?" she asked, wiggling her powerful shoulders.

The tiny pony laughed in a whinnying kind of way. "Of course there is. Your wings!"

Luckily, with her new long neck, Eloise could easily turn to look. Just as the pony said, on her broad back was a pair of wings. Huge ones!

"Try them out," the pony urged.

"Um... I don't know how to fly," Eloise replied. She felt nervous all of a sudden.

"Just give it a try," the pony said kindly, flapping its own wings and rising into the air. "You'll soon get the hang of it."

But Eloise wasn't quite ready. So much had happened, she needed a moment to adjust.

"First, can you please tell me what's going on?" she asked. "Where am I? And who are you?"

"My name is Sparkles," said the pony, landing daintily back on the ground. "And this is the Magic Forest. You've been called here by the Tree Queen. She's the ruler of the Magic Forest."

Magic Forest? Tree Queen? It felt like every question raised ten more! Sparkles seemed to sense Eloise's confusion.

"I'm to take you to the Tree Queen's glade,"

she added. "She'll explain everything to you. And she'll tell you about your quest."

Eloise's heart skipped. She was going on a quest? She really wasn't sure how she felt about that. If Ash and Maya were here, she might feel different. But going on a quest alone felt scary.

"Is it possible that the Tree Queen has made a mistake?" Eloise asked. "I'm not at all sure that I'm a Fire Dragon." She laughed. "I'm not very fiery."

Sparkles tossed back her mane and fixed Eloise with her deep blue eyes. "You're definitely a Fire Dragon. I can see it in you. But sometimes that inner flame takes a while to reach full strength."

Eloise nodded, but she didn't really know what this meant.

"Okay, let's try out that flying," said Sparkles, rising into the air once more. "We need to get going before we are spotted."

Spotted by who? Eloise thought, but she decided not to ask.

Instead, she took a deep breath and flapped her wings. It was a strange feeling—like discovering she had an extra pair of arms. But to her surprise, she lifted off the ground.

"See? You can do it!" Sparkles said, galloping in midair. "Keep flapping."

Eloise did, and soon found herself doing slow circles in the air.

"You're a natural!" Sparkles cried.

"I don't know about that!" Eloise laughed.

But at the same time, she had to admit that flying was fun. She just hoped she wouldn't have to fly too high. It was way less scary when she was close to the ground.

"Are you ready to get going?" Sparkles asked, after Eloise had completed a few more moves. The little horse looked around her, snorting. "I think we're being watched. Can you feel it?"

Eloise could indeed feel it. Just the vague sense that someone or something was nearby.

"That means Chaos Critters are in the area," Sparkles explained, lowering her voice. "They've been in the Magic Forest before, but they've changed form since we last saw them. Now they are stranger and more powerful than ever."

Eloise had no idea what a Chaos Critter was, of course. But she could tell from Sparkles's tone that they were not nice.

She nodded. "I'm ready," she said in her bravest voice. "Lead the way!"

3

To Eloise's relief, Sparkles flew fairly close to the ground. All the same, it wasn't easy keeping up with the little pony. She galloped expertly between the trees at top speed, her gray mane and tail streaming out behind her. Eloise made sure not to lose sight of the pony. She didn't want to be left behind!

From what Eloise could tell, the Magic Forest was huge, stretching out in every direction. Even though it was warm, the air was filled with lovely woodsy scents. Eloise could smell fresh grass and blooming flowers and ripe fruits. But there was another smell in the air, and this one was unpleasant. It took Eloise a moment to recognize what it was.

"Is something burning?" she called out to Sparkles. She hoped the Magic Forest wasn't on fire!

Sparkles looped back and flew next to Eloise. "That's not burning you smell," Sparkles murmured. "It's the Fire Realm. It only appears every thousand years. The smell means something is wrong with the realm." Her voice dropped lower still. "We think the Chaos Queen is involved."

Eloise had no idea who the Chaos Queen was, but she could tell from the name that she wasn't someone good. She shivered.

"We must hurry," urged Sparkles. "I can sense the Chaos Critters are getting closer all the time."

The little pony flew higher now, leading the way above the treetops. Eloise was nervous about flying up here. But she was more worried about running into these Chaos Critters, whatever they were!

"There's the glade!" called Sparkles, pointing

a silver-gray hoof. "You can see the force field around it."

When she looked, Eloise saw a very strange thing: a barrier of shimmering air. That must be what Sparkles meant by force field. Through the fuzziness, Eloise could see the outlines of trees and flowers. There also seemed to be some large creatures flying around in there.

"I can see more dragons!" Eloise gasped.

"Yes, they're the other Fire Dragons," Sparkles explained. "Hey, don't look so worried! I am *sure* you'll like them."

Eloise hoped Sparkles was right. It usually took her a while to warm up to new people. Even with Ash and Maya, it had taken a while.

This was mostly because Eloise worried that she wasn't cool enough or fun enough. But maybe it would be easier with dragons?

"Are you coming in with me?" Eloise asked Sparkles hopefully.

Sparkles shook her head, ruffling her mane. "I'm sorry, I can't. But I'll come and find you whenever you need me." With a kick of her hooves, Sparkles galloped away.

Eloise steadied herself. The sooner she entered the glade, the less time she had to worry about what was going to happen. Pressing her wings to her sides, she dove toward the force field. The shimmering air tickled her scales as she passed through it and into the glade beyond. The air here was cool and the grass was soft beneath her paws as she landed.

"Great work!" said a dragon, clapping two front paws.

"I did a triple somersault when I landed," said another dragon, walking over, too. "And not on purpose."

Eloise's heart leapt. She would know those voices anywhere. "Ash? Maya? Are you both Fire Dragons, too?"

A moment later, she found herself caught up in a wing-hug.

"Yes! Isn't this incredible?" said the first dragon, who had Ash's voice.

"I've always wanted to go on a magical adventure," said the one with Maya's voice. "Going on one with you two makes it even better."

Eloise nodded. Having her two best friends here changed everything. "Where is the Tree

Queen?" Eloise asked, suddenly remembering what the little pony had told her.

"I'm here," said a warm, rich voice.

Eloise spun around to see the large tree in the center of the glade transforming into an elegant woman. She wore a flowing green robe and her brown hair tumbled over her shoulders. Eloise stared, too amazed to speak.

The woman raised her arms. "I am the Tree Queen, protector of the Magic Forest," she said. "And I am very grateful to you three for coming here. The Magic Forest has fallen on difficult times. Are you willing to help?"

Eloise's heart beat very fast, but she nodded without hesitation. So did Ash and Maya.

The Tree Queen gave a small, grateful smile. "Tell me, do you know anything about the Fire Realm?"

"Only that it appears every thousand years," Eloise said. "It's here now, but something is wrong."

The Tree Queen nodded slowly. "The Fire Realm is a very mysterious part of the Magic

Forest. Most of the time it is invisible. When it does appear, very few forest creatures can enter it. You three are among the few who can. It's very hot in the realm, but you'll find you don't mind the heat. This is why I need your help."

"I could smell burning on the way here," Ash commented.

Maya nodded. "It smelled bad."

"That's how we know something is amiss," the Tree Queen said gravely. "The Fire Realm should not smell like that. And this hot, still air isn't right. Things are all topsy-turvy now."

"Because of the Chaos Queen?" asked Eloise.

Ash and Maya looked at her in surprise.

Eloise knew why. Normally, Eloise didn't like speaking up or asking questions. But somehow, being in dragon form made her feel braver.

"We suspect so," the Tree Queen said, looking at Eloise with her wise brown eyes. "Normally, the Fire Realm appears when it is time to appoint a new leader of the realm. I am worried that the Chaos Queen has plans to meddle with this—which could mean terrible things for the forest."

"Why would this Chaos Queen want to do that?" Ash asked, looking outraged.

The Tree Queen sighed. "She thrives on chaos. She was brought under control by another team of Dragon Girls. Unfortunately, she found a way to break free. Chaos always does in the end. If I am right, then she is furious about what happened, and plans to cause as much chaos as she can. Messing up the Fire Realm is the perfect way to achieve this."

4

The Tree Queen gazed at the three Fire Dragons, her expression serious. "This will be a dangerous and challenging quest. Do you accept it?"

Ash and Maya nodded immediately. After a short pause, Eloise nodded, too. Going into a fire realm and fighting a queen and her critters all sounded very scary. But she wouldn't be doing it alone.

The Tree Queen turned to Eloise. She reached a long branch-arm toward her. On it was a drawstring pouch made of soft gray velvet. "I would like you to lead this quest," she said. "Take this. I have a feeling it will come in handy."

Hastily, Eloise backed away. "Ash or Maya would be better at leading," she said.

Slowly but firmly, the Tree Queen shook her head. "You have what is needed for this quest," she said. "I know it, and your friends know it. You just need to believe it yourself."

"You can definitely do this," said Ash.

"And we'll back you up the whole time," added Maya.

Eloise reached out a paw and took the bag, slinging it around her neck. Everyone else seemed sure that she could lead this quest. Maybe, just maybe, they were right?

"What do we have to do?" she asked, hoping no one would notice the wobble in her voice.

But something strange was happening to the Tree Queen. She was flickering between looking like a human and looking like a tree. "Unfortunately," she said, her voice growing faint, "I have only received small flashes of information from the Fire Realm. I know they were preparing for their new leader's arrival. I also know that something is stopping this from happening. But what the exact problem is, I can't be sure."

Eloise's chest tightened. Leading a quest was one thing. But leading a quest when you didn't know what to do was quite another!

The Tree Queen's voice was soft like whispering leaves. "My advice is to search for the Forever Flame. It is a vital part of the new leader ceremony. I can feel in my roots that something is wrong with it."

"Okay," Eloise said. This wasn't much, but it

was something at least. "And how do we get to the Fire Realm?" Eloise had seen how vast the Magic Forest was.

The Tree Queen looked entirely like a tree now, and Eloise feared she wouldn't reply. But then she flickered back into her human form.

"The Fire Realm moves," she said. "It could be anywhere. All I can tell you is that right now, it feels very far away. Use your senses, Eloise. They'll guide you."

With that, the Tree Queen's human form disappeared and did not return.

Eloise felt nerves crash over her like a wave.

"Don't worry," said Ash, wrapping a wing around her. "We'll figure it out."

"Together," Maya added, joining in with the wing-hug.

Eloise managed a small smile. She hoped her friends were right!

They flapped their wings and rose into the air. Eloise wished she could stay in the safety of the glade. But the Tree Queen had asked her to lead a quest and so that was what Eloise would do.

Side by side, the Fire Dragons shot through the shimmering force field and back into the strangely warm air of the forest. As they rose higher, Eloise was surprised to see Ash and

Maya weren't perfect at flying, either. Ash almost crashed into a tree. And Maya somehow kept flipping upside down as she flew. But neither of them seemed worried about it. In fact, they were both laughing.

"Flying is sooooo hard!" said Ash, swooping to avoid a branch.

"It is," Maya called back. "But it's also really fun. I guess we'll get the hang of it in the end."

"Hey, Eloise, which way should we go?" asked Ash.

Eloise's heart did a little jump. Should she know that? The Tree Queen had said to use her senses. But which ones? She certainly couldn't *see* the way. She couldn't *taste* or *feel* it, either. And all she could hear were forest sounds: birds singing, insects buzzing, leaves rustling. What sense did that leave? Her sense of smell!

Lifting her dragon snout, Eloise breathed in

deeply. She could smell... smoke! That should lead them to the Fire Realm.

Eloise sniffed again. It was as though the scent rolled out before her like a ribbon, twisting through the trees.

"This way," she said to her friends.

On and on the Fire Dragons flew. But Eloise barely noticed the distance. She simply focused on following the scent. The deeper into the forest they went, the stronger the smell of smoke became.

Eloise was so intent on tracking the scent that she didn't notice how much better their flying was getting. But her friends did.

"Look at this!" said Ash, shooting forward and doing a midair roll that was only slightly wonky.

"Check me out, too!" cried Maya, doing a dragon-shaped cartwheel.

Eloise whooped. Could she do those tricks? She felt like maybe she could. But just as she was about to try a cartwheel, Eloise spotted something that made her stop. Her friends very nearly crashed into her.

"What is it?" Ash asked.

Wordlessly, Eloise pointed.

Up ahead was a wall. It stretched up and out in all directions, completely blocking the sky and any glimpse of forest beyond. Coming across a wall in the middle of this wild place was strange enough. But what was even stranger was that it was entirely made of flickering, twisting flames.

The Dragon Girls flew toward the flaming wall, the fire crackling and warming their faces. When they were very close, they landed. Eloise stared at the flickering flames. What should they do now?

A little mouselike creature popped its head out from a nearby bush. Eloise expected it to run away when it saw them. Surely three huge dragons would be terrifying to such a small animal.

But the mouse hopped over on its back legs like a tiny kangaroo! "Greetings, Fire Dragons. Welcome to the Fire Realm," it said, twitching its long whiskers. "We've been waiting for you."

"You have?" Eloise glanced at her friends, surprised.

"Of course," replied the mouse. "You've come to help with the Sudden Blooming."

Eloise didn't know what to say. She had no idea what the Sudden Blooming was, and she was pretty sure Ash and Maya didn't, either.

The little mouse didn't seem to notice their confusion. "My name is Bernie," he continued cheerfully. "I'm a Fire Hopper, as you can probably tell by my lovely strong legs. Come on. I'll show you the way to the field where the blooming happens. Or where it *should* happen, at least."

With that, Bernie turned and started hopping toward the blazing wall.

"Careful! Stop!" yelled Eloise as Ash and Maya gasped in horror. "Stay away from the fire!"

But the little creature paid no attention and, with an elegant bounce, hopped right through the flames.

A moment later, Eloise could see him faintly on the other side, waving a paw at them through the fiery barrier.

"Come on!" he called, his little voice somehow rising above the crackling of the flames. "You're Fire Dragons, aren't you?"

Eloise, Ash, and Maya turned to one another.

Eloise could see that for once, her friends were just as unsure as she was.

"We might look like Fire Dragons," muttered Ash, "but we're ordinary kids on the inside."

"Exactly," said Maya. "Fire is really dangerous. Flying into a wall of it seems like a bad idea."

Eloise didn't know what to do. Her friends were right, of course. But they also had a quest to complete. And the queen did say they could enter the Fire Realm.

She felt a fluttering from above and turned to see Sparkles approaching.

"Don't worry," whinnied the little pony. "You'll be perfectly safe. Your scales are fireproof. In fact, flying through the fire wall will make you stronger."

Eloise felt herself relax, confident that Sparkles would never lie to her.

"The Tree Queen asked this of us," she reminded her friends, "so it must be possible. Let's fly through at the same time?"

Ash and Maya nodded, and together, the Dragon Girls flew into the wall of flames.

The fire felt like the air of a hand dryer against Eloise's scales—warm and strong, but not painful at all. Eloise felt power tingling through her. It was just as Sparkles had said!

They landed on the other side, laughing

excitedly at what they had just done. It was even hotter on this side of the wall.

"Sparkles! Look at you!" Eloise exclaimed.

The pony's fur and wings were aglow with golden tones. Her mane and tail were bright red and orange.

"I'm not the only one who has changed," said Sparkles.

Eloise looked around at her friends. Her jaw dropped. They looked completely different. They were still dragons, of course, but now Ash was a beautiful shiny blue and Maya was a rich scarlet. They both had a flamelike pattern on their scales.

"You two look amazing!" said Eloise.

"So do you!" cried Ash and Maya.

Eloise looked down at herself. Sure enough, her gray scales were now a gleaming golden color, with the same flame pattern as her friends! Even the plain velvet pouch the Tree

Queen had given her was now covered with the fiery motif.

"All creatures that can pass into the Fire Realm transform once they do so," explained Sparkles. "Our fiery sides really come out when we're here, in our element."

Eloise was not sure she had a fiery side. But she had to admit she felt good. It was like she was buzzing with energy.

"See? I told you it'd be fine," said Bernie the Flame Hopper, who was now bright orange. He jumped up onto Eloise's shoulder. "Let's go to the Fire Field. I'll show you the way."

As they flew along, Eloise gazed at the

landscape below. The Fire Realm seemed huge. In some ways it was a lot like the rest of the Magic Forest, with trees, grass, flowers, and birds. But here the trunks of the trees glowed red hot, and flame-shaped leaves fluttered from their branches. The grass also looked like tiny flickering flames in shades of red, yellow, and orange instead of green. Eloise spotted a bird flying toward them with a long tail of fire and a flickering crest. As it passed them, the bird left a glowing streak of light in the air.

But despite all the fire, the Fire Dragons didn't feel uncomfortable. Eloise decided this must be what it was like for people who loved really, really hot weather. She could feel that it was superhot, but it didn't bother her.

"Look!" cried Bernie. "There's the Fire Field. That's where the Sudden Blooming should take place."

Eloise saw what appeared to be a field of giant matchsticks, poking up out of the ground. Eloise grimaced. She didn't like matches. And she definitely didn't like fields of giant ones.

Bernie directed Eloise to land, and soon all three Fire Dragons were staring at the strange matchsticks. They were almost as tall as the dragons.

Eloise wished she could fly off in the other direction. *But I'm leading the quest*, she reminded herself.

There was a rustling, and a group of Flame Hoppers appeared. They bounced over to the Dragon Girls excitedly, all talking at once.

"Thank goodness you're here!"

"Did you hear the Forever Flame has been stolen?"

"The Sudden Blooming should have happened already!"

Eloise started to feel overwhelmed from all the information and all the bouncing. She held up a paw. "Please, one at a time. Can you explain what the problem is exactly?"

Bernie took over. "What my friends are trying to say is that the Forever Flame is gone. It normally burns atop Candlestick Tower. But it has vanished. Without it, the Match Blossoms can't open."

The smallest Fire Hopper whispered, "And that means no Sudden Blooming, which is a disaster."

Eloise's mind began to churn. "Is there any other way to make the Sudden Blooming happen? I mean, without the Forever Flame?"

"Actually," said Bernie, hopping higher than ever, "there might be a way. But it's never been done before. You'd need to collect the most magical and fiery ingredients to act like the Forever Flame. Mixed together, they might be powerful enough to start the Sudden Blooming."

Eloise liked the sound of this. It reminded her of baking. Her friends looked interested, too.

"So, what are these ingredients?" Ash asked.

"And where can we find them?" Maya added.

Bernie shrugged. "You're the Fire Dragons. You'll figure it out."

Before Eloise could ask any of the questions swirling in her mind, she noticed a drop in the temperature. It was suddenly almost cool. She was about to turn when something hit the back of her neck, exploding into liquid. It felt like a water balloon, but filled with warm slime.

"Chaos Critter attack!" yelled the Fire Hoppers, bouncing away in all directions. "Watch out!"

6

Eloise had no idea what to do. She looked over at Ash and Maya. Uh-oh! Two stonelike objects were heading right for them!

"Duck!" she yelled, but she was too late. The gray lumps smashed into Ash's back and Maya's shoulder. Instantly, the lumps burst into sludge that oozed across her friends' scales. As the liquid hit the ground, it sizzled slightly, before re-forming into lumps and shooting back up into the sky. Soon the critters were hurtling toward them again.

Eloise's nervous jitters grew. How were they going to defend themselves against these awful things?

Sparkles appeared beside Eloise. "Don't let them see your fear," she whispered. "And try flying above them. These Chaos Critters are full of slime and too heavy to fly very high."

"Follow me!" Eloise called to Ash and Maya as she whooshed into the air. From down on the ground, the Chaos Critters had looked like a looming hailstorm. A strange and magical mist swirled around them, like it was protecting them from the heat of the realm. But with only a few flaps of their powerful wings, Eloise, Ash, and Maya were above the nasty creatures.

The Chaos Critters chattered furiously and flung themselves upward at the Fire Dragons. A few managed to smash against their scales, but with much less force.

Eloise felt a tickle in her throat. Was it a cough? She opened her mouth, and a roar exploded from her! It was loud and swirled with golden flames.

The Chaos Critters screeched and backed away from the blast of sound and heat.

"Go, Eloise!" cheered Ash.

"I didn't know you could do that!" said Maya, her eyes wide.

"I did," Sparkles said, looking at Eloise proudly. "I could see the fire in you, just below the surface!"

Eloise felt a flutter of pride. She really was a Fire Dragon!

Suddenly, Ash cried, "They're coming back!"

The Chaos Critters had regrouped and were zooming this way.

This time Eloise's roar was louder—and hotter. The golden flames whirled around the critters and broke through the cooling air protecting them. They squeaked in fury as they disappeared into the distance.

"That was amazing!" said Ash.

But the roaring had made Eloise dizzy. Her vision blurred and the world tipped.

"Are you okay?" Maya called as Eloise began tumbling toward the ground.

"Flap your wings!" Sparkles called urgently.

Eloise did, managing to slow her fall but not

stop it completely. She landed with a small *splat* on the ground.

"I'm fine," Eloise assured her friends as they landed beside her, their faces full of concern.

In fact, Eloise was better than fine. She was actually quite comfortable. Whatever she'd landed on was very soft. She looked around and saw she was surrounded by big puffy flowers.

"They're like dandelions when they go to seed," commented Ash.

"I love blowing on those and making wishes," added Maya. "Sometimes I can get all the seeds off with one breath."

Eloise loved doing that, too, watching the

fluff whirl away on the breeze. These Fire Realm ones were much bigger and fluffier. And they were bright orange.

Eloise felt another tickle, but this one was in her nose. Was she allergic to the flowers? The tickle grew and grew until...

Achoo!

As a huge dragon sneeze exploded from Eloise, several dandelions burst into a shower of sparks.

"Whoa!" Ash said, her eyes wide.

"They look like tiny fireworks!" Maya gasped.

A thought occurred to Eloise. Perhaps these flowers would be good in their potion? They certainly seemed to catch fire easily. Carefully, she snipped off a couple of the firework flowers with her sharp talons and placed them in the pouch the Tree Queen had given her.

Hopefully the flowers wouldn't explode while they were in there!

"Good thinking," said Sparkles, swishing her tail. "Your instincts are strong and your inner flame is getting brighter all the time. I'll return if you need me." With a toss of her fiery mane, Sparkles galloped off.

Eloise was sorry to see her go. She liked having the pony nearby.

When she turned around, Ash and Maya were looking at her expectantly. Eloise felt her chest tighten. That's right—she was leading the quest! "So, I guess now we go searching for other ingredients for our potion," she said.

"Let's," Ash agreed.

"Which way?" Maya asked.

It was a very good question, and Eloise didn't have a good answer. "Let's just explore," she suggested. "Just keep one eye out for ingredients that might work in our potion."

"And keep the other eye out for Chaos Critters!" Ash added.

The three Fire Dragons soared back into the air and began exploring the Fire Realm. It was an extraordinary place. They saw huge flocks of birds with fluttery flame-wings, and deer with fire-tipped antlers. Eloise even spotted a squirrel with a flickering fire-tail.

In the distance, they could see mountains that glowed pink-red. With so many fiery things about, it should've been easy to collect more ingredients for their potion. But somehow nothing felt quite right to Eloise. Everything seemed either too big or too small or not quite magical enough.

And then a crackling sound made Eloise's ears prick up.

7

Ahead, Eloise saw strange lines of fire squiggling through in the air. They were constantly changing shape. One moment they were circles, then they were spirals, then zigzags. It reminded Eloise of swirling sparklers on a dark evening. But these lines were brighter.

"What are they?" Ash asked as they flew closer.

"I think they're... insects?" Maya said uncertainly.

As they approached, Eloise saw that they were indeed insects. It was a swarm of large, stripey wasps. But instead of wings, they had flickering flames to fly with. Eloise shuddered. She didn't like wasps—and ones with fire for wings seemed even worse.

At the same time, there was something about them that captured her attention. What were they doing?

The Fire Dragons slowed down, and cautiously

drew nearer. The wasps began zooming back and forth in front of them.

"We're Hot Wasps," the wasps announced in high, buzzy voices. "You look fun to sting. Mind if we try?"

Normally, a swarm of wasps would have sent

Eloise running indoors—especially ones that were suggesting they try stinging her. But she was a dragon, and she was feeling braver all the time. Also, she was distracted by an interesting scent. Something hot and spicy. Eloise wasn't a huge fan of spicy food, but this smelled really good.

"We're here to find ingredients for a potion," Eloise explained to the Hot Wasps, ignoring their stinging comment. "It's to make sure the Sudden Blooming happens. Can you tell me, what is that smell?"

"It's the Burning Berry Bush!" the Hot Wasps replied. "We are its protectors. Just one drop of its juice can cause a fire."

"That sounds perfect for our potion," Ash said, flying closer—but not too close—to the wasps.

"We need to find things that we can use to replace the Forever Flame," explained Maya.

"Burning Berry juice would definitely help with that," the Hot Wasps agreed, flying in pleased zigzags.

"May we pick one, then?" asked Eloise. "It's for the good of the Fire Realm."

"Yes, yes, go ahead!" buzzed the Hot Wasps. "It makes perfect sense. We'll make a tunnel for you to fly through."

Their flame-wings fluttered and burned.

"You won't sting us, will you?" asked Eloise.

"Unfortunately, we can't promise that." The wasps sighed. "We'll try not to. But you know how it is when you're a wasp. Most of the time we just can't resist."

"If we do sting you, they will only be friendly, encouraging, little stings," the wasps added reassuringly.

Eloise, Ash, and Maya exchanged a look. Eloise was pretty sure there was no such thing as a friendly sting!

"I say we forget about the berries," whispered Ash, who clearly felt the same way. "It's just one ingredient. I bet there are plenty of other things we could use."

"I agree," Maya whispered back. "I don't trust these Hot Wasps. They don't even trust themselves."

Eloise surprised herself by shaking her head. "I have a strong feeling that we need one of those berries," she said. "It's something about the way they smell. I'm going to get one, but I'm going on my own. There is no point in all of us risking being stung."

Ash and Maya stared at her. "Are you sure?" Ash asked. "It seems dangerous."

"And maybe painful," Maya added.

Eloise smiled at her friends. "It'll be fine," she said, hoping it would be. Eloise turned to the

Hot Wasps, who were now drawing bright arrows in the air. "I'm going to pick a Burning Berry," she told them.

The wasps formed a giant corkscrew shape in the air. "Just fly through this tunnel," they buzzed. "It'll guide you right there."

"We'll try not to sting you too much," they added.

Eloise took a big gulp of warm air, smiled at her friends again, and flew into the burning tunnel of wasps. Almost immediately a wasp darted at her, stinger ready. As carefully as she could, Eloise brushed it away with her tail. Another wasp darted at her from a different angle. This time she surged forward, managing to dodge its attack. Unfortunately, she didn't spot the third wasp, which snuck up from behind.

"You're doing great!" it said as it stung her.

To Eloise's relief, the sting didn't hurt too much. Clearly, heat wasn't the only thing that Fire Dragons were protected against! Now that she knew the stings hardly hurt, Eloise stopped worrying about the wasps. Sure, it was annoying to have them constantly darting at her, but at least it wasn't annoying AND painful.

As she flew through the tunnel, the spicy smell grew stronger. Eloise could see something glowing at the end of the tunnel: a low bush with long brambles curling out like a waterfall. *Or*, thought Eloise, *like a spider with way too many legs*. Each of the brambles dripped with bright little fruits. *Burning Berries!*

"Well done!" cried the wasps, stinging her faster in their excitement. "You're almost there."

With a final flap of her wings, Eloise popped out of the fiery spiral. She was surrounded by bushes of Burning Berries. The moving spiral was rustling the plants, and every time the glowing fruits hit one another, a shower of sparks was released into the air.

Eloise landed and surveyed the bushes,

searching for the best-looking berry. She spotted one low to the ground, bright and full of juice.

"Good choice," buzzed the wasps.

But just as Eloise reached out a claw to pick it, she felt a familiar flutter by her side.

"Be careful!" Sparkles warned. "Burning Berry Bushes are very jumpy."

Jumpy? What did that mean? Eloise soon found out. With a loud pop, the bush leapt right out of the ground and lunged at her.

Eloise turned to fly away from this horrible spiderlike plant. But in her haste, she stumbled and fell. The plant leapt on her, wrapping her up in its thorny brambles.

"Let me go!" Eloise yelled, struggling to get free. But the more Eloise wriggled, the tighter the plant gripped her.

The Hot Wasps flew around in wild squiggles. "We tried to protect you, we really did!" they said.

"Hang on," Eloise panted as she twisted this way and that, "isn't your job to protect the Burning Berry Bush from being attacked?"

"No, it's actually the opposite," the Hot Wasps

buzzed. "Our job is to protect everyone from being attacked by the bush!"

Eloise really wished the wasps had mentioned this earlier. She would have prepared herself! The plant's sharp thorns were digging into her and she kept getting splattered by Burning Berry juice. Luckily, her scales were tough, but, all the same, it wasn't very pleasant.

"Eloise, don't worry. We'll help you!"

Looking up, Eloise saw the most wonderful sight. Ash and Maya were flying through the wasp tunnel, dodging their stings!

"Don't get too close. This bush is nasty," she warned her friends as they burst out of the tunnel.

At this the bush growled and sprouted new brambles, which it threw around Eloise.

Ash and Maya hovered in midair, clearly uncertain of what to do. Eloise was uncertain, too! But something had to be done—and quickly. She was so tightly wrapped now, she couldn't move at all.

She heard Sparkles's gentle voice in her ear. "The Burning Berry Bush is not only jumpy, it's also very prickly," the little pony said.

"That's for sure!" Eloise groaned.

"I mean its personality," Sparkles said. "It gets offended easily. I suspect it was mad that you didn't ask before trying to pick one of its berries. If you speak to it kindly, it calms down.

But you must mean what you say. If you give it a fake compliment, it gets even more prickly."

Could this be true? Eloise's dad often talked to the indoor plants when he was watering them. He said it made them grow better. Maybe talking to plants really was helpful. But what compliment could she possibly give this angry, thorny bush? She opened her mouth, hoping that some smart words would come out... but instead, a drop of Burning Berry juice dropped in!

Eloise had assumed that the berries would taste hotter than the hottest chilis. They had the power to start fires, after all. But the juice in Eloise's mouth wasn't overly spicy. It was sweet, tangy, and delicious.

"Wow! Burning Berry juice tastes great!" Eloise said. Instantly, she felt the brambles loosen a little.

The Hot Wasps buzzed happily.

"That was good," Sparkles whispered. "Keep going."

Eloise thought quickly. What else could she say that was kind and true? "The moment I saw you, I knew that your berries would be perfect in our potion. It's obvious that you've got a lot of magical power."

The bush made a funny sound, like a

satisfied sigh. Some of the brambles fell away, and Eloise was able to free her legs.

Ash and Maya had been watching and caught on. "We've only just gotten here and already we can see how strong you are," Ash called, still hovering at a safe distance.

"And...um..." It looked like Maya was struggling to think of a nice thing to say.

Eloise held her breath, hoping Maya wouldn't say anything to make the plant angry. "And you've got such shiny thorns!" Maya finished.

Eloise had to try hard not to giggle. It was a weird compliment, for sure. But the Burning Berry Bush seemed to like it. Then she thought of something very important to say. "I really should've asked before trying to take one of your berries. That was rude, and I'm sorry. If you'll allow us to have one, I promise that we'll put it to a good use."

With a little shake of its leaves, the bush unwrapped itself from around Eloise and replanted itself in the ground, using its leaves to gently pat the earth in around its roots. Then it rustled its leaves once more, and Eloise saw something fly into the air.

It was the big berry she'd spotted earlier.

"Catch it!" her friends shouted as the bright fruit spun through the air, sending out a shower of sparks.

Eloise leapt up and neatly caught the fruit in

one outstretched paw. Ash and Maya cheered as Eloise landed and safely tucked the berry into the velvet bag.

"Feel free to drop by any time you need an encouraging sting!" the wasps called as Eloise flew up to join her friends in the air.

"Thanks!" Eloise said politely. But to her friends she whispered, "Come on, let's go." Prickly plants and stinging wasps were not exactly her idea of fun.

Soon, the Fire Dragons were back in the sky, streaming through the Fire Realm. Flying didn't seem nearly so hard now that they'd had so much practice. Eloise found she didn't have to concentrate as hard.

This was lucky, because she had plenty of other things to think about. Like their potion! This was clearly on Ash's and Maya's minds, too.

"Do you think we have enough ingredients?" Ash asked.

Eloise had been wondering the same thing. "I feel like we need one more thing," she said. "But I don't know what."

"Maybe some twigs?" Maya suggested. "Whenever I go camping with my family, we always collect lots of kindling for our campfire. You can never have too much."

Eloise thought about what they had collected so far: the firework flowers and a Burning

Berry. Maya was right! Twigs would be the perfect last ingredient. The only question was where to get them. She scanned the ground below. There were plenty of trees, but somehow none of them felt quite right.

Her eyes stopped on the river winding its way through the landscape. It was the color of molten gold, and heat rose from it in waves. Halfway along, something was blocking the flow of water.

"I think that's a dam," said Ash, who was looking at the same thing.

"Like the ones beavers make back home," Maya added. "That will be filled with twigs, but they'll be all wet, of course. And wet twigs don't burn."

"But this is the Fire Realm," Eloise reminded her. "And that is clearly no ordinary river. Let's go and look!"

9

The moment they landed by the side of the river, Eloise knew that her hunch was right. The river wasn't filled with water at all—at least, not the water she was used to. This river ran with something more like a syrup. It was thick, golden, and bubbly. Fire water!

"It looks like caramel sauce," Maya said.

Ash carefully dipped in a claw and then licked it. "It tastes a little like caramel sauce, too," she reported. "Want to try it, Eloise?"

Eloise didn't reply. She was too focused on the dam they'd spotted from the air. It was indeed made of twigs, and the fire water was lapping at the branches. Eloise moved closer. She felt certain that fire water would make the twigs more powerful.

But could they just take a twig or two? After her experience with the Burning Berries, Eloise was wary. The last thing they needed was some angry Fire Beaver to attack them for ruining their dam.

Sparkles flew up beside her. "It's okay," she said. "This dam has been abandoned. You can tell by all the gaps in it. It's fine to take twigs from it."

Eloise reached out and pulled one of the twigs free. As she tucked it into the velvet pouch, a prickle of nerves ran up her spine.

The breeze was cooler all of a sudden, and she could feel danger in the air.

Sparkles could feel it, too, and whinnied a warning. "Look out! Chaos Critters!"

Eloise felt the familiar *splat* of a critter exploding into goo across her back. Was she imagining it, or was the liquid even hotter this time? Glancing up, she saw many more of the creatures whooshing toward them in their protective mist. Another gray blob hurtled toward her, narrowly missing the velvet bag with all the precious ingredients.

"We've got to get up high," she called.

Eloise and her friends had worked hard to get the ingredients for their potion. There was no way she was going to risk having them destroyed now.

Flapping her wings as hard as she could, Eloise surged into the sky, with Ash and Maya close behind. The Chaos Critters screeched and flung themselves at the Fire Dragons with all their might, smashing into liquid. It was like being caught in the middle of a terrible hailstorm—but one where the hailstones re-formed after they smashed apart, only to attack once more.

Even worse, the Chaos Critters seemed bigger and more furious than ever.

It was hard to fly with all the critters pelting her, their hot and gooey liquid coating her wings. Eloise tried to roar them away but ended up with a mouthful of the horrible slime. Instantly, the dizziness Eloise had felt during the last critter attack returned. Her head swirled and her vision grew foggy.

From behind, Eloise heard a cry. She turned and saw something that made her angry. Really angry. A mass of Chaos Critters were attacking her friends from every side.

Eloise didn't even feel the next roar coming. It just burst from her in an eruption of sound and flames, filling the air with brilliant golden heat. Instantly, the mist evaporated and half the Chaos Critters were flung away in a whirl of heat and noise. When Eloise roared again, with even more force, the remaining critters turned and fled.

"Wow, that was amazing!" Ash called out as she and Maya flew over, each wrapping a wing around Eloise.

"Truly next level," Maya agreed. "I didn't know you had that in you."

"Neither did I," Eloise said. "But I really don't like it when I see my friends getting picked on."

"Well, we're lucky to have you as our friend!" Ash laughed.

"Totally," Maya said. "But that was true even before you roared those overgrown water balloons away."

Eloise felt herself smiling from one dragon-y

ear to the other. It was so nice to hear her friends say these things. She always worried that she wasn't as fearless as they were. It was wonderful to feel like the bravest one for a change.

Sparkles tapped Eloise with one of her little golden hooves. "Don't forget about the quest!"

Of course! They still had to make the potion and return to the Match Blossom field. And they didn't even know if the potion would work!

"Let's land," Eloise said to her friends, leading the way to a clearing not far from the Fire River. The three Fire Dragons sat in a circle, surrounded by fluttering Flame Trees. Eloise's mind raced as she opened up the bag. She had been so focused on collecting ingredients that she hadn't really thought about the next step. How would they actually make this potion?

When she looked into the bag, she groaned in dismay. "I don't understand. Everything's gone!"

She couldn't believe it. The pouch was completely empty. The ingredients must have fallen out somehow.

"It's not your fault," Ash said, although her voice wobbled a little. "It must have happened during that critter attack."

"We'll just have to collect the ingredients again," said Maya.

Eloise felt Sparkles by her side. "The ingredients aren't gone," she said. "They've just made something new."

Something new? Eloise looked into the bag again. The ingredients had definitely disappeared, but now there was something she hadn't noticed right at the bottom. Carefully, Eloise pulled it out. It looked like some kind of rock, flat on one side and with a rough surface like sandpaper.

"I think it's a striking stone," Sparkles said, reaching out a hoof and touching it. "I've never actually seen one before. When you roared away the Chaos Critters before, the ingredients must have turned into the exact thing you need."

Eloise frowned. "But we're trying to create something to replace the Forever Flame," she said. "This rock is nothing like a flame."

"It isn't," agreed Sparkles. "But if it's a striking stone, it will still start the Sudden Blooming when you rub it against the Match Blossoms."

Suddenly, Eloise understood. "Like striking a match against the side of a matchbox?"

"Exactly!" Sparkles neighed as she galloped into the air. "Now, follow me. There's no time to lose."

As they flew back toward the Fire Field, Eloise gave herself a pep talk. She wanted to stay calm, but she really didn't like striking matches. How was she going to set a whole field of giant matchsticks fire?

I'll figure out a way, she told herself. *This is really important.*

It wasn't long before Eloise saw the tall plants on the horizon. She patted the velvet bag, making sure she could still feel the stone within.

Sparkles looped back and flew alongside her. "Are you ready?"

"Not really," Eloise admitted softly, her pulse racing.

There seemed to be even more matchstick plants than before. *Maybe Ash or Maya can do the striking*, she thought. But then she shook the idea away. The Tree Queen had put her in charge of the quest. It really was her job to finish.

Her friends sensed her worry.

"You can do this," Ash said.

"You absolutely can," agreed Maya. "Since we've been in the Magic Forest, you've done so many brave things."

"Your friends are right," said Sparkles. "That inner flame of yours is burning very brightly now."

Eloise realized, with a flash of pleasure, that this was true. She had roared away Chaos Critters. She had battled prickly plants. She had even flown through walls of fire and tunnels of wasps. Lighting up some Match Blossoms was nothing!

Without another word, Eloise took the striking stone from the bag and flew lower. When she reached the first tall stem, she hovered in midair. Then, gripping the stone in her paw, she struck it against the top of the blossom.

Instantly, a beautiful flower burst open. Flame-shaped petals in gorgeous tones of orange, red, and gold glowed in the light

Eloise felt Sparkles nudge her. "Now, roar on it!"

She did as the little pony said, roaring loudly. The single bloom flared and bent slightly, touching the stick nearest to it. That one burst into bloom, and lit the next stick and the next. A warm perfume began wafting through the air.

The Dragon Girls cheered.

"You did it!" Sparkles clapped her front hooves. "Let's fly up high. The Sudden Blooming is best viewed from above."

She was right. Looking down on the Fire Field as the blooming spread was an amazing sight.

"It's like dominoes," marveled Ash as each one touched the next and blossomed.

"Burning ones," Maya said, laughing.

Once the entire field had bloomed, Eloise turned to Sparkles. "Should we head back to the glade?"

She couldn't wait to tell the Tree Queen what they had achieved. The quest had seemed so big and impossible at first. But they'd done it!

Sparkles nodded. "It's time."

Side by side, the Fire Dragons flew toward the wall of flames that protected this strange, fire-filled part of the Magic Forest. This time Eloise didn't hesitate before flying through it.

The little boost of power it gave her was just what she needed for the long return flight.

"Our fiery colors have disappeared," Ash said, a little sadly.

Eloise saw that the others' scales—and her own—had indeed returned to a pale gray.

"That may be true," Maya said, "but our wings are as good as ever."

As if to prove it, she flew higher and began doing midair stunts. Of course, Ash and Eloise had to join her. Together, they twisted, looped, and spun their way back to the glade, little Sparkles neighing and galloping alongside them. The scent of burning was still in the air, but Eloise was certain she could smell the Match Blossoms now, too.

When they reached the shimmering force field, two very different feelings swirled inside Eloise. She was really proud of completing the quest. But she was sad that their time in the forest would soon be over.

At least I got to come here, she reminded herself. *How many people get to do that?*

Ash and Maya raced through the hazy, magical air of the force field. Eloise hovered on the spot, pausing to give Sparkles a hug.

"Thanks so much for all your help and encouragement," she said.

"It was an honor to go on this quest with you,"

Sparkles replied, whinnying softly. "It was also really fun! Goodbye for now, Flame Dragon."

With a final swish of her mane, the little pony cantered off across the sky. Eloise watched until she had vanished from view, then, tucking her wings against her sides, dove through the force field.

Her friends cheered as she landed on the lush grass beside them.

"Here she is. The quest leader!"

"Who even needs a Forever Flame when you've got an Eloise?"

Under her scales, Eloise felt herself blush. And she grew even warmer when she saw the Tree Queen beaming at her.

"Dear Flame Dragon! You had so much doubt when you arrived. But I always knew that you could do it. How brave you can be when you trust yourself! And look how good at solving problems you are."

"It wasn't just me," Eloise pointed out. "We did it together."

The Tree Queen nodded. "I know. And a very fine team you three make. Which is why I hope you'll return to help me with the next stage of this quest."

"There's another stage?" Eloise cried. She had thought this was the end!

"There is," said the Tree Queen. "The Fire Realm is waiting for its new leader to emerge.

The Sudden Blooming is the first part of the process. But the Forever Flame is still missing, so I need your help for the second step. Will you return?"

Eloise didn't need to look at her friends to know that they were nodding just like she was.

"Wonderful," said the Tree Queen as she began to sway.

At first Eloise thought she was returning to her tree form. But instead, little blossoms fluttered from the queen's highest branches. As they fell, they burst into flickering pink flames that smelled faintly of warm apple pie. The blossoms swirled around the Fire Dragons, warm but not hot, moving faster and faster until Eloise couldn't see anything other than flaming pink flowers.

Eloise closed her eyes and felt herself lifting off the ground, then gently floating back down again.

Cautiously, she blinked her eyes open. She was back in her living room at home, staring at the table with the cake on it.

There was a moment's pause while Eloise tried to pull together her thoughts.

"We found the matches!" announced Maya, bursting back into the room.

"And I've got your present," said Ash, coming down the hall.

Eloise turned to her friends, feeling dazed.

Had they really just been fiery dragons, flying around in the Magic Forest?

Then Ash winked, and Eloise was sure. It had really happened!

Maya handed Eloise the matches. "Want a turn after all?" she asked with a smile.

Eloise nodded, and, to her parents' surprise,

she carefully struck a match and began lighting the candles. "After you've both had a turn blowing these out," she said, "I'm going to cut us enormous slices of cake. I have a feeling you two are just as hungry as I am." Now it was Eloise's turn to wink at her friends. "I guess that's not surprising, though. We've been flying around all day!"

Turn the page for a special sneak peek of Ash's adventure!

DRAGON GIRLS

Ash the Blaze Dragon

1

Ash watched the flames of the crackling campfire leap and dance. She often went camping with her family. She especially loved the evenings around the fire. This trip was extra special because her friends Eloise and Maya were here!

Earlier, Ash and her friends had helped set

up the tents. They had a big one while her dad was sharing the smaller one with Ash's little brother. After the tents were set up, Ash, Maya, and Eloise had made theirs extra cozy with cushions and rugs they'd brought from home. Then they'd sat inside and painted their nails together. Ash chose bright blue, Maya red, and Eloise gold.

When the sun began to set, Ash had made a campfire for them to sit around.

"Ooh! I think my marshmallow is ready," Eloise said. She took her stick out of the flames and pulled off the toasted treat. "SO good," she said, her mouth full of gooey sweetness.

Ash poked with a blue fingernail at the

marshmallow at the end of her own stick. "A few more seconds," she decided, holding the stick over the fire again. She liked her marshmallows to be exactly right. "But Maya, quick! Yours is about to—"

The white blob at the end of Maya's stick dropped into the fire. In seconds, the marshmallow bubbled away to nothing.

"Not again!" Maya half groaned, half laughed. "That's the third one that the fire has eaten."

"Here, you can have mine," Ash said. She held hers out to her friend. Her marshmallow was perfectly cooked now.

Maya smiled and shook her head. "That's so nice, but you have it. I don't even like marshmallows very much. It's all about toasting them."

"Really? I love them," Ash said. "But I hate the way they make my fingers all sticky."

As Ash popped the marshmallow into her mouth, her dad crawled out of the smaller tent. "Jack is finally asleep," he said. Then he nodded approvingly. "Campfire looks good, Ash! You must have been taught by an expert."

Ash rolled her eyes. "As you know, YOU taught me!"

Every time they went camping, Ash and her dad were in charge of constructing the perfect fire. Ash knew how to gather the right kindling and logs. She always scrunched the paper super small and arranged everything so it all burned perfectly.

"Like I said, you must have been taught by an expert." Her dad winked. As he spoke, a spark jumped out of the campfire and flickered against the dark sky. "Looks like a fire-breathing beast, doesn't it?" Ash's dad commented. "Not that I've ever come across one, of course."

Ash, Maya, and Eloise exchanged secret smiles. They knew exactly what fire-breathing beasts looked like. In fact, they knew what it felt like to *be* a fire-breathing beast!

Recently, the three friends had found themselves in a place called the Magic Forest. In this realm, they became Fire Dragons. It wasn't just that they could breathe fire. They also had a special connection to all things fiery.

Ash and her friends had already completed one quest for the Tree Queen, the ruler of the forest. Now they were waiting for the queen to call them back to help again. Ash couldn't wait!

Ash's dad made the girls peach tea, heating the water over the fire. As they sipped the fragrant drinks, the girls chatted and sang songs and told ghost stories. At least, they tried to tell ghost stories. Somehow, the tales all ended up being more funny than scary. Ash had never laughed so much! She'd always loved camping, but doing it with friends was even more fun.

Finally, Ash's dad stretched and yawned.

"Bedtime, everyone. Ash, could you put out the fire?"

Ash picked up the bucket of water they always kept nearby. She sloshed the water over the glowing coals. With a hiss, a cloud of steam rose into the air. Once it cleared, Ash's dad checked the coals carefully.

"All out," he confirmed. "Good night, you three. Tomorrow morning we'll build a brand-new fire to cook breakfast on."

Ash, Maya, and Eloise squeezed into their tent, still laughing and chatting as they got ready for bed. Ash was an experienced camper, so she got changed quickly and hopped into her sleeping bag. But her friends found it much harder.

"Can someone shine a flashlight over here?" Eloise asked. "Something weird is going on with my pj's."

"Same!" Maya muttered. "I think mine have shrunk."

Ash found her flashlight and clicked it on—then burst out laughing. Eloise's top was inside out *and* upside down. And somehow Maya had managed to squeeze both of her legs into just one pajama leg. The friends helped one another out, and soon everyone was snuggled into their sleeping bags.

Just as she closed her eyes, Ash heard a noise from outside the tent. It sounded like the crackling of flames. She frowned. Strange!

"I'm just going to check that the campfire really is out," she told her friends. She slipped out of the tent, zipping it up behind her.

The fire was out, and the pit was still damp with water. But as Ash watched, a strange blue flame leapt into the air. Ash knew that blue flames were usually the hottest. But this flame produced no heat.

Ash wasn't surprised. She'd already guessed that this was no normal flame. It had a silvery shimmer to it, for one thing. And for another, Ash could hear soft singing floating from it.

Magic Forest, Magic Forest, come explore...

DRAGON GIRLS

#1: Azmina the Gold Glitter Dragon

#2: Willa the Silver Glitter Dragon

#3: Naomi the Rainbow Glitter Dragon

#4: Mei the Ruby Treasure Dragon

#5: Aisha the Sapphire Treasure Dragon

#6: Quinn the Jade Treasure Dragon

#7: Rosie the Twilight Dragon

#8: Phoebe the Moonlight Dragon

#9: Stella the Starlight Dragon

Collect them all!

#10: Grace the Cove Dragon

#11: Zoe the Beach Dragon

#12: Sofia the Lagoon Dragon

#13: Hana the Thunder Dragon

#14: Mina the Lightning Dragon

#15: Zora the Snow Dragon

Special Edition: Rani the Enchanted Dragon

DRAGON GAMES

PLAY THE GAME. SAVE THE REALM.

 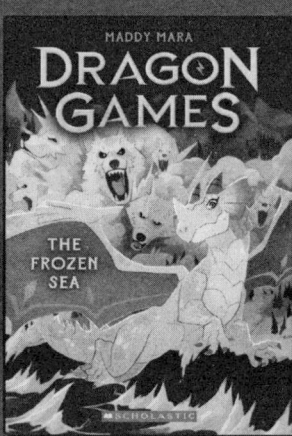 

READ ALL OF TEAM DRAGON'S ADVENTURES!

Forever fairies . . . and forever friends!

READ THEM ALL!

FOREVERFAIRIES
SCHOLASTIC and associated logos are trademarks and/or registered trademarks of Scholastic Inc.

SCHOLASTIC
scholastic.com

ABOUT THE AUTHORS

Maddy Mara is the pen name of Australian creative duo Hilary Rogers and Meredith Badger. Hilary and Meredith have been making children's books together for many years. They love dreaming up new ideas and always have lots of projects bubbling away. When not writing, Hilary can be found cooking weird things or going on long walks, often with Meredith. And Meredith can be found teaching English online and all around the world or daydreaming about being able to fly. They both live on the lands of the Wurundjeri people in Melbourne, Australia. Their website is maddymara.com.